KEEPER

ANN EVANS

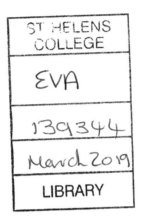
Keeper ISBN 978-1-78464-708-7

Text © Ann Evans 2017
Complete work © Badger Publishing Limited 2017

Publisher: Susan Ross
Senior Editor: Danny Pearson
Copyediting: Cambridge Publishing Management Ltd
Designer: Bigtop Design Ltd
Cover: İbrahim Süha Derbent / Alamy

2 4 6 8 10 9 7 5 3 1

CHAPTER 1
RARE BREEDS

Robyn clasped her hands over her mouth, wanting to be sick. It was vile – and so very wrong.

'Leave it Fudge!' she cried, as her dog went in for a closer look.

Clipping the lead back on to Fudge's collar, she backed away.

It had been a sheep, one of her Uncle Joe's. But only its blood-covered fleece was left. The flesh had been torn from its bones. And the bones crushed and broken.

Robyn's mind raced. What had done this? Not a fox, not a dog. Not even a pack of dogs. They couldn't snap bones into splinters.

Her grey eyes darted left and right. Afraid in case whatever had done this was still around. She swept Fudge up into her arms.

Far across the field, the rest of the flock stood huddled together. Watching.

'We need to tell Uncle Joe!'

Setting her dog down, they raced towards the farmhouse.

Breathless, she found her uncle raking hay in a barn. Even with his back to her, he looked angry. He was always angry at something. Perhaps he already knew about his sheep.

'Uncle Joe?'

'Robyn?' he snapped. 'What are you doing here?'

She took a deep breath. 'One of your sheep has been killed....'

He swore then slammed the rake down, making Robyn and Fudge jump.

'Not another one!' he raged, his face turning red. 'Third time in a month!'

'Oh no!' She dodged aside as he stormed past her. 'What's doing it?'

He marched across the yard and into the farmhouse. She followed.

'Bloomin' new people,' he ranted, unlocking a cupboard. He took out his shotgun and cartridges. 'Rare breeds! I'll give them rare breeds....'

Robyn gaped, horrified, 'What are you doing?'

'They're keeping something vicious,' he snarled. 'And it's getting out and eating my sheep.'

'You don't know that,' Robyn cried, jumping aside again as he grabbed his truck keys.

'I know my sheep weren't being butchered before they came.'

'Uncle Joe!' She raced outside after him. 'Uncle Joe, wait!'

He started the truck's engine. Robyn scrambled in too, Fudge on her lap.

He turned and glared at her. 'You get off home.'

'No way! I'm coming with you. In the mood you're in, you might end up killing someone.'

He stamped on the accelerator. 'You're not wrong there!'

*

As they bounced along the country lane, Robyn knew where they were heading. A mile away some new people had bought a house and land – then put up high fences all around it. All the locals were talking about them. They were foreign. They kept animals, rare breeds. That was as much as anyone knew.

'Uncle Joe, you're going to look silly if they only keep goats and pigs.'

'Goats and pigs, my backside!' he growled. 'I'm telling you, it's something vicious.'

'Well even if it is, you can't go shooting it,' Robyn argued.

Muttering to himself, Joe turned sharply up a lane marked 'Private'.

Robyn spotted the big old house. The high wooden fences all around it looked new, as did the barbed wire along the top.

'Looks like they don't want people breaking in,' said Robyn.

'Or breaking out,' said Joe, turning the engine off. With his shotgun open and hooked over his arm, he marched up to the front door.

With Fudge on her lead, Robyn ran after him. 'Uncle, you shouldn't bring your gun!'

Ignoring her, he rapped on the door loudly. It was ages until it opened.

An elderly man and woman stood there. He was small and coffee coloured. She was thin and looked so tired. Robyn thought that once she must have been very beautiful. But now she looked like she had all the worries of the world on her shoulders. Finding a gun-toting angry farmer on the doorstep wouldn't help.

Her fearful eyes locked on to the shotgun. She grasped the man's arm.

He stepped forward. 'What do you want?'

'Something is killing my sheep!' Joe snapped. 'One of your animals is getting out and ripping them to pieces.'

'Not possible!' said the man.

But Joe wasn't giving up. 'I want to know what you're keeping. You'd better show me or I'm calling the police.'

The couple flashed warning looks at each other. Then the woman spoke. Her accent was East-Asian. 'Come and see. All of the animals are safe in their cages. All locked up.'

Uncle Joe marched into their house like he owned it.

'Sorry,' Robyn said to them, feeling awful.

The man nipped ahead, barring the way. 'Please leave your gun here!'

Robyn saw the look in his eye. A look of steel. And even though he was old and small, he stood his ground. Finally, Uncle Joe took out the cartridges, and stood the gun in a corner.

The man led the way to the rear of the house. Outside it was all concreted, with cages and wooden buildings, like a small zoo.

'OK, so what do you keep?' Joe demanded.

The woman waved her arms. 'Go have a look. You will see it is all safe.'

Joe didn't need telling twice. But as Robyn went to follow, Fudge dug in her paws, not wanting to go anywhere but out of here.

Robyn picked her up. She was trembling.

'Hold on to your dog tightly,' the woman said.

'Aren't you coming, too?'

They both shook their heads.

'Our daughter, Sheena, is the keeper,' said the man. 'She will see to you.'

'OK,' Robyn said, settling Fudge down first. With a lot of fuss, she was walking on her lead again. 'Silly girl, the animals are locked up. Nothing can hurt you.'

As she wandered around, Robyn saw how true that was. There were rabbits, goats and chickens. They didn't look like special rare breeds, but then what did she know?

The pathway curved into a horseshoe shape. At the bend was a large cage of monkeys. There was nothing to say what breed they were, but they were cute and funny.

She felt lucky to have a mini zoo all to herself. She stood there watching, enjoying their antics. Until, suddenly, she felt something – sensed something close. Fudge barked – a warning bark as Robyn felt a warm breath on her neck.

CHAPTER 2
A PRIVATE ZOO

Robyn spun round and gasped in surprise. Beautiful, almond-shaped, honey-brown eyes were fixed on her. 'Oh!'

The girl was about her age, with smooth dark skin and hair that shone like black silk. And when she smiled, she had the most perfect white teeth ever.

'Hello,' she said. Her voice was soft.

Robyn felt tingly inside. 'H… hello.'

'I am Sheena, the keeper. Who are you?'

She had the same accent as her mother, and Robyn felt totally tongue-tied. The girl was tall, slim and perfect. And that silky, purring voice sent shivers through her body. 'Er, I'm Robyn. My uncle….'

The girl, Sheena, bent down to stroke Fudge. 'Who is this?'

'Um… Fudge….' Fudge had rolled on to her back. 'Oh! That's odd. She usually jumps up at everyone.'

Still crouched, Sheena smiled up at Robyn, making her tummy do a double flip.

'I like your dog. She is sweet.'

'Yes… yes she is. Look, I'm sorry we've barged in….'

Sheena stood upright. She was inches taller than Robyn. Her smile seemed full of love. 'What does your uncle want?'

Robyn felt hot. This girl had a way of looking at her…. 'Well, my uncle Joe thinks one of your animals has got free and is killing his sheep.'

Sheena raised her eyebrows. 'Nothing has escaped. I would know.'

'Yes, I'm sure. Anyway, you don't seem to have anything dangerous.'

Sheena's honey-brown eyes glinted. Robyn saw a wicked gleam. 'Ah, we do. Our pets are from Malaysia. From the jungle.'

Robyn stared at her – which wasn't hard. Sheena was gorgeous. And the way she made her feel was… strange. There were girls at school whom she liked. But compared to Sheena, there was no contest.

Trying not to let her mind wander, she said, 'So, what animals do you keep?'

Sheena curled one finger. Her nails were long and polished gold. 'Come with me. I will show you.'

Robyn's heart thudded as she followed Sheena into a large wooden building. The girl moved gracefully, hips swaying.

The room was warm and dark. At the far end was an area lit up behind glass. Fudge had dug in her heels again, so Robyn scooped her up, eager to see what was behind the glass.

There was a large shallow pool, with rocks and driftwood. And half in, half out of the water was an alligator. It was so still it looked unreal.

'He is handsome,' purred Sheena.

The memory of that dead sheep flashed into Robyn's mind. 'What does it eat?'

'Not your uncle's sheep!' Sheena laughed.
It was a nice sound, and Robyn found herself laughing, too.

She pulled a face. 'Sorry!'

They stood watching the alligator doing nothing for long minutes. Every now and then Sheena ran her finger over Fudge's head – but smiled into Robyn's eyes.

'Come!' she finally said. 'You can meet Pele.'

'Who's Pele?'

Sheena just smiled.

Out in the daylight, there was no sign of her uncle. Perhaps he'd calmed down. Hopefully he was having a cup of tea with Sheena's parents.

They went into another wooden building. This, too, had a glass wall with rocks and bits of wood behind it. And curled around a thick branch was a huge snake.

'A python!' Robyn gasped. 'It's massive!'

'Pele is five metres long,' Sheena said, watching Robyn's face.

'Wow! Is he dangerous? Would he hurt us if he got out?'

She laughed again. 'He won't hurt me. He might hurt you. You and your dog would be in big trouble if he got out.'

Robyn held her pet closer. The thought of Fudge ending up in a python's stomach horrified her.

'It is OK,' said Sheena. 'He will not get out.'

Robyn liked Sheena's wicked sense of humour. She seemed to find it funny to scare her. Well that was OK. She could take a joke, especially when the joker was as gorgeous as Sheena.

'Keep the dog on the lead.' She stroked Robyn's arm as she turned and walked away.

'Oh!' Robyn couldn't hide her disappointment. 'Do you have to go?'

'Yes. You can stay. Keep looking at our pets. You will like them.'

With a sigh, Robyn watched her go. It would have been nice if Sheena had hung around, chatted. They could have got to know each other more. With another sigh, Robyn went out into the sunshine.

Fudge was still jittery, even near small animals. It was a shame there were no information panels to read. But this was a private zoo. She really was lucky getting to look around.

Walking back towards the house again, Robyn stopped in her tracks.

Ahead was a huge cage. A tangle of tree trunks formed a climbing frame. A tractor tyre hung from a chain and there was a high wooden platform. It looked like a lion's den.

Fudge began to panic – whining and pulling madly on her lead.

There was no sign of a lion or tiger, but Fudge could probably smell it. Robyn scooped her up again. 'It's OK. It can't hurt you.'

Then her heart skipped a beat. Padding slowly from a tunnel at the back of the cage came a magnificent, sleek, black panther.

Its coat gleamed like black velvet. Its beautiful head swayed from side to side, sharp amber eyes fixed on to her and Fudge instantly.

Fudge whimpered.

Robyn could not drag her eyes off it. It was beautiful, perfect – and very, very lethal. It paced back and forth. Eyes bright, muscles rippling, black coat gleaming.

Robyn stood in awe.

Then a harsh voice at her side snapped, 'That's it!'

Robyn glanced at her uncle. He hadn't calmed down. He looked red and angry. He jabbed his finger at the black panther.

'That's what's killing my sheep.'

Robyn almost laughed. 'You are joking! If this got out it would cause a riot!'

'I'm telling you. This is what's eating my sheep.'

'Uncle Joe, you've lost three sheep in a month. This can't have been free for a month. Someone would have spotted it.'

'It hunts in the night.'

Robyn shook her head. 'Then finds its way home, like a pussycat?'

His face twisted. 'Maybe someone brings it home.'

'What!'

'It must cost a fortune feeding this lot. Lead the panther to some free meat, save them some cash.'

Robyn shook her head. 'That's crazy….'

'Well my sheep didn't rip themselves to bits!'

'No, I know that,' Robyn said, trying to calm him

down. 'Look, let's go and find Sheena. She'll put your mind at rest.'

'The keeper?' he grumbled. 'She's keeping her head down. I haven't set eyes on her yet.'

'She's lovely,' Robyn said, hoping he wouldn't read any more into it. Just like her parents, her uncle believed girls should marry boys, boys should marry girls, have kids, all nice and straightforward. Well, maybe she would marry one day, but it wouldn't be to a boy.

They searched, but Sheena wasn't about. Finally, they returned to the house. Sheena's parents opened the door to them.

'That panther!' Joe snapped, pushing past them. 'You're letting it out, aren't you?'

'No!' the woman shouted. 'We keep it locked up!'

'Well I want to check those locks….'

'I have an idea,' came a smooth, purring voice.

Robyn swung round as Sheena walked in through a door. It looked like a cupboard door, but Robyn saw a corridor beyond it. For a second, she wondered where it led. But then Sheena was at her side and her thoughts turned to mush.

'Er, Uncle Joe, this is Sheena,' she stammered.

'Uncle Joe,' Sheena repeated, which seemed to annoy him even more. 'You believe the panther got out of its cage?'

'Yes! Yes I do!'

'So, we shall do a test. I will lock you in the cage and see if you can get out.'

'Are you mad?' Joe raged.

Sheena winked at Robyn. 'He would quickly find a way out!'

Robyn tried not to smile. Sheena really did have a wicked side.

Joe's face was so red he looked ready to explode. He grabbed his shotgun and strode to the door. 'You haven't heard the last of this! Robyn – home!'

She cast Sheena a shy smile. 'It was nice to meet you.'

Sheena touched her arm. 'I would love you to come back.'

'Sheena, no!' her mother said sharply.

Robyn bit her lip. The woman had seen it – the attraction between them. She didn't approve. Like everyone else.

But Sheena ignored her mum. 'At the weekend, Robyn?'

'Sheena!' her dad warned.

Sheena turned her back on them both. 'Please!'

Robyn sensed that Sheena wanted to kiss her. She was so close, her red lips parted.

'Sheena!' both parents shouted. And then the woman grabbed Robyn by the arm and pushed her out of the door.

'At the weekend!' Sheena shouted, and then the door slammed shut.

CHAPTER 3
FEEDING TIME

The week dragged. School was dull. People were dull. Even her friends felt dull. They were all a pale shadow compared to Sheena.

Fudge was back to normal, which was good. Uncle Joe had got rid of the dead sheep's fleece. And none of his other sheep had been attacked.

A normal week, and Robyn felt like it would never end. She counted the hours until Saturday. At last it came. She had butterflies in her stomach.

'Aren't you taking Fudge with you?' her mum asked, as she set out.

'No,' said Robyn, kissing the top of Fudge's head. 'She doesn't like it there. She can smell the animals. Anyway, I'm going on my bike.'

Her mum looked worried. 'It is safe, isn't it – this zoo?'

'Yes, all the animals are behind bars.'

'People have been talking,' her mum went on. 'Why come all the way from Malaysia? Why have a zoo that isn't open to the public?'

'I don't know,' Robyn shrugged, keen to get going. 'They love animals I suppose.'

'You know, Robyn, people have been talking… Mrs Lea from the post office, she read a really odd story on the internet….'

Robyn groaned. 'She is such a gossip!'

Her mum followed her outside. 'So, what will you be up to today?'

Robyn got her bike from the shed. 'Just chatting. Maybe I'll help feed the animals – well, the friendly ones.'

'You will be careful….'

'Yes! I'll see you later!'

She set off before her mum could ask any more questions. Honestly! People were so suspicious! Sheena and her parents simply loved animals. What was so wrong with that?

Cycling down the lane, she wondered how Sheena's mum and dad would greet her. They had been so unfriendly last week, pushing her out of the door. What if they didn't even let her in today? What if they sent her packing without Sheena even knowing she was there? If only she'd got her phone number. She could have called and said she was on her way.

Well, it was too late now. As Robyn rode up the private lane, she had a sinking feeling that the parents were going to be difficult.

Propping her bike by the fence, she knocked on the door. There was a noise – like scuffling – and voices. Maybe they were holding Sheena back. But surely they wouldn't be that strict? But what did she know of different cultures?

And then the door opened, and Sheena stood there, smiling.

'You came!' Sheena said, her white teeth shining like pearls. And then her face dropped. 'Oh! Where is your dog?'

The disappointment on Sheena's face shocked Robyn. It was like she was more interested in Fudge than in her!

She tried not to let her hurt pride show. 'Well, she was so jittery last time, I've left her at home.'

Sheena's parents came into the hall.

'Come in, Robyn,' said her mum. 'Would you like a drink?'

'Yes please,' said Robyn, surprised at how nice the woman was being today.

They led her into the living room. It looked very drab. It needed decorating. The furniture looked like old stuff left by the people who had lived there before. There was nothing Oriental, not a rug or a vase. It looked as though they'd brought nothing with them from Malaysia – except the animals, of course.

Sheena's mum came back with juice and biscuits.

'Thank you… aren't you having any, Sheena?'

Sheena pulled a face, but then watched her as she ate and drank, not saying a word. While the parents watched Sheena – like hawks.

No one spoke. The mood seemed heavy. Robyn was glad when her new friend suggested they go and look at the pets.

'It's nice that you call them your pets,' said Robyn, once outside. 'Not just animals.'

'They are pets – well… most are,' said Sheena, as they headed to the rabbits' cage. She had a bunch of keys on her belt. She took one and opened the lock.

Robyn fussed the rabbits while Sheena refilled their feeding bowls. 'Are these special breeds? I used to have one that looked just like this.'

Sheena scooped one up and held it close to her lips, as if she was going to kiss it. 'Ah yes, these are very special! I love rabbit!'

'Rabbits,' Robyn corrected her.

Sheena smiled and her white teeth glinted. 'Yes, rabbits.'

'So, why did you come to England?'

Sheena's golden eyes narrowed. 'You ask a lot of questions.'

She hadn't meant to be nosey. Just trying to make conversation. 'I'm just curious. You know, you could open the zoo up to the public. People would pay to see your… pets.'

'Good idea, Robyn.' Sheena's red lips curved. 'I like this idea. It sounds like fun.'

Robyn noticed that the old couple were still watching from a little way off. They looked tense.

'Do your parents…?' Robyn stopped herself. 'Sorry, that was another question.'

Sheena cast her a look that was almost a warning. Then said, 'My parents – what?'

'I just wondered if they liked it here. Have they settled in? They seem a bit worried about you.'

Sheena locked up the rabbits again, then slid her arm through Robyn's. 'They always worry about me.'

While her heartbeat thudded at their closeness, Robyn saw that Sheena flashed a wicked smile back at her parents. As if trying to wind them up.

They walked slowly on, arm in arm, Sheena's parents 100 metres back, like chaperones. Not leaving them alone for a second.

'Do you have a boyfriend?' Robyn asked. 'Whoops, sorry – another question!'

'No. I do not like boys.'

'Nor me,' Robyn said, her hopes rising. Although there was no chance of the parents approving of any relationship that might spring up between them.

As they strolled from cage to cage, Robyn tried to learn about Sheena's life in Malaysia.

'Do you miss living in Malaysia?'

'Yes,' she said, spreading her arms and twirling round and round suddenly. 'I was free in Malaysia! I could run and play in the jungle. It is a beautiful country.'

'So why come here, to England? I'm glad you did, by the way.'

Sheena slid her arm through Robyn's again. Robyn had never felt so happy. She just hoped her new friend was happy, too.

'If I tell you, you would not believe me.'

'Try me!'

Sheena looked for a moment like she was about to give away some big secret. Then changed her mind. 'No. I will not tell you.'

Robyn began to understand. 'Were your parents in some kind of trouble in Malaysia? Did they have to leave?'

Sheena's golden eyes widened. 'This is true. You are a very clever girl!'

'Had they broken the law?'

'Yes. Correct again.'

Robyn recalled her mum talking about an odd story on the internet. Maybe they were linked. She would ask her mum later. But right now, all that mattered was that this lovely girl was holding on to her arm, and smiling at her.

'Do you not have any more questions?'

Robyn shook her head. 'I don't want to pry. You can tell me more if you want to.'

'You are a sweet girl,' Sheena said, her lips moving close to Robyn's cheek. 'You even smell sweet!'

'Thank you!' It was a nice thing to say. But Robyn couldn't return the compliment. Sheena had a kind of earthy smell. Maybe because she worked with animals. It was nice though.

'OK, so I'll tell you,' said Sheena. 'My Mummy and Daddy are scientists.'

Robyn shot her a look, surprised she called them Mummy and Daddy. It seemed a bit babyish.

Sheena went on. 'They created a new thing. People didn't like it. They made us leave.'

Robyn's eyes were wide. 'What did they create?'

'It is a secret. Anyway, you would not believe me.'

'I might.'

Sheena shook her head. 'No, it would not be a good idea if I told you.'

'OK,' shrugged Robyn. She wasn't that interested in her parents. She just loved hanging out with Sheena. 'Could we see the black panther again?'

'She is probably hungry now. It is feeding time soon.'

'Oh, that would be great to see!' Robyn said, eagerly.

They walked on, with Sheena stopping at each

cage to feed the animals. But when they reached the panther's cage, there was no sign of it.

'I expect it's in the back,' said Robyn.

Sheena threw back her dark head and laughed. 'Of course! Or in Uncle Joe's field eating his sheep.'

'Oh! Don't say that!'

'I'm hungry, too,' Sheena said, walking away. 'We should go into the house.'

'What about feeding the panther?'

'She can wait.' And then she looked back at her parents, who were still keeping an eye on her, and shouted, 'I am hungry! I need food!'

It seemed such a rude way of asking if dinner was ready. But she saw the parents quicken their step, as if used to following orders. Perhaps Sheena's bossy manner was her way of getting her own back on them for not giving her any freedom.

The parents joined them in the kitchen. Sheena peered into the fridge, moving food about but not eating anything. Her mood had changed. She seemed restless.

'We are going to eat now. You need to go home, Robyn,' said the woman.

'Oh!' Being asked to leave surprised her. If Sheena had been a guest in her house, she would have been invited to stay and eat. Different customs, she guessed. 'Well, OK. It's been nice seeing you, Sheena.'

The girl didn't answer, her mood was getting blacker by the second. She paced back and forth across the kitchen floor, looking in cupboards but not finding anything she wanted to eat.

'Go now!' the woman said again, louder.

It was like before: Robyn was rudely pushed out of the door. Only this time Sheena wasn't looking like she wanted to kiss her goodbye. She seemed to have forgotten all about her.

Sheena's dad ushered her towards the front door. 'Goodbye, Robyn!'

As he opened the door, they both rocked on their heels.

Uncle Joe was marching towards them, gun over his arm and looking madder than ever.

CHAPTER 4
THE LAST STRAW

'Robyn, go home!' Uncle Joe raged. Then jabbing his finger at Sheena's dad, shouted, 'And you stay right where you are!'

'What's happened?' Robyn asked, but had a horrible feeling that she already knew.

'Another sheep killed! Butchered! Eaten!' Uncle Joe ranted, pushing Robyn out of the way and storming through the house. She ran after him.

Sheena's mum seemed to shrink into her skin. Clearly, this was another bit of bad news that she could do without. The last straw.

Sheena, however, looked ready to do battle. Her black mood lifted. She pulled back her shoulders, looking taller, defiant. Her head held high, and her eyes sparking with a warning glint.

'That blasted black panther's been out on the hunt again. Don't deny it. There was a witness.'

'Must have been a dog,' the woman argued, the colour gone from her face. Her eyes wild and frightened.

'This was no dog,' Uncle Joe said, barging past all of them and striding outside. 'I'm getting the police on to you!'

'Uncle Joe!' Robyn cried.

'Go home, Robyn!' he yelled at her.

She went to run after him, but Sheena barred her way. She calmly held up her hands. 'Stay here. I will deal with Uncle Joe!'

'Sheena!' Her mum's cry came out as a wail.

It was such an awful sound that Robyn turned and stared at the woman. She sank down on to a chair, head in her hands, and began weeping. Her husband looked just as distressed. He went to his wife and put his arms around her.

They clearly thought Uncle Joe was going to shoot the panther. It so obviously meant the world to them. They'd brought it all the way from Malaysia. It was their pet. Robyn could just imagine if someone wanted to shoot her dog.

'He won't shoot it,' Robyn promised, and ran out after Uncle Joe and Sheena.

They were way ahead, Uncle Joe ranting and raging, Sheena walking calmly alongside him. But Robyn knew her uncle wouldn't be charmed by a pretty face. His sheep were his livelihood. He couldn't allow the killing to go on.

Yet Robyn just could not believe that Sheena and her parents would be so stupid as to let a panther go out hunting. This was the English countryside, not a jungle....

Then Sheena's words leapt into her head – *'I was free in Malaysia!'*

Robyn wondered if that meant free to allow her panther to go out hunting. Was that how the parents were breaking the law? Was that why people out there were getting angry with them? Why they had to leave?

It all started to make sense.

*

She ran after them, past the cages. The animals were restless, picking up on her uncle's anger. Rabbits and chickens scuttled about, monkeys screeched and leapt frantically from branch to branch.

Hurrying around the horseshoe bend she saw them at the panther's cage.

Uncle Joe marched right up to the bars, gun pointed and ready to shoot. Then he turned angrily on Sheena. Robyn could hear his words from where she was.

'What a surprise! It's not there!' he raged.

Robyn heaved a sigh of relief. Glad it was in the back den, out of reach. Out of danger.

'Still out hunting, is it?' he yelled. 'Gone walkies? Comes back on its own, does it?'

'No,' said Sheena. Her voice soft and purring. 'It is here.'

Her uncle was red in the face. 'Show me then!'

Robyn stood still. She'd never seen her uncle so mad, while Sheena seemed to be enjoying every second.

'I said show me!'

He had his back to Robyn, but Sheena had spotted her. She looked right at her. Amber eyes glinting. Robyn gasped.

Those eyes….

And then Sheena began to writhe, to squirm, her slim body twisting and turning, her colour changing. Darkening. Her head widened, her nose became bigger, her long hair spread right over her body, until her clothing vanished and a black rippling sheen covered her from head to toe.

Uncle Joe dropped his gun in fright. He staggered, gasped for breath.

Sheena's eyes grew larger, but still that bright and dangerous gleam shone from them. Her mouth widened. Her teeth grew. Two white fangs glinted in the sunlight.

And then she dropped to the ground. No longer standing, but on all fours, snarling – a beautiful and deadly black panther.

CHAPTER 5

BEAUTY AND THE BEAST

Robyn's feet were riveted to the spot. Her scream locked in her throat, terror and shock making breathing almost impossible.

Her mum's words ran through her head. *'Mrs Lea… from the post office… read a really odd story on the internet….'*

What had Sheena said? *'My Mummy and Daddy are scientists. They created a new thing. People didn't like it. They made us leave.'*

She saw her uncle scramble for his gun. But Sheena was quicker. She pounced. Jaws wide open. Snapping them shut around Uncle Joe's neck.

The sound of crunching bone was sickening.

He didn't scream. Didn't make a sound. It was just so quick.

And as her poor uncle lay in a pool of blood, Sheena – her lovely friend Sheena, this evil, monstrous creature – began to eat him.

The scream that had been locked in Robyn's throat erupted. She ran at the beast, snatching up the shotgun, which was sticky with her uncle's blood. She took a step back, the gun pointing at the black panther.

And then, in the next second, the panther began to writhe and twist and squirm. The black hair shot up from the animal's body, forming long tresses on its head. And the head changed back into the beautiful face of Sheena, while the body shimmered back into the shape of a beautiful girl.

Sheena stood there, wiping blood from her lips with her fingertip. 'No one will ever believe you, Robyn. You are just a lonely girl. They will say you are mad if you tell anyone.'

Tears sprang into Robyn's eyes. 'And they'll never believe a girl like me could shoot a beautiful girl like you.'

She struggled to hold the gun steady. It was so heavy, and her body trembled.

'You will not shoot me, Robyn,' said Sheena. 'You love me.'

She was right. Her heart ached. But her poor uncle lay dead on the ground. And who would be next? Her school friends, her family, her dog, her?

Sheena crept forward, smiling still, arms outstretched.

Robyn didn't know whether those arms were to hold her, or take the gun from her – or to rip her to pieces.

It had to be now! *Pull the trigger!* her mind screamed.

Her finger twitched on the trigger, but refused to pull it.

'See,' purred Sheena. 'You cannot kill the one you love….'

'Yes you can!' screamed Sheena's mother, rushing at them. In a flash, the woman's arms were around Robyn, reaching for her hand. Robyn felt the pressure and strength forcing her finger down on the trigger.

'Mummy!' Sheena screamed.

The sharp crack of gunfire sent the birds screeching.

And then all was silent.

ABOUT THE AUTHOR

Ann Evans lives in Coventry in the West
Midlands. She has written around 25 books,
including the award winning *The Beast*. One of
her most recent titles is *Celeste*, a time slip thriller
set in her home city. Her Teen Reads and Dark
Reads titles are *Nightmare*, *By My Side*, *Red Handed*,
Straw Men, *Kicked Into Touch* and *Living The Lie*,
Ann also writes magazine articles on all kinds
of topics.